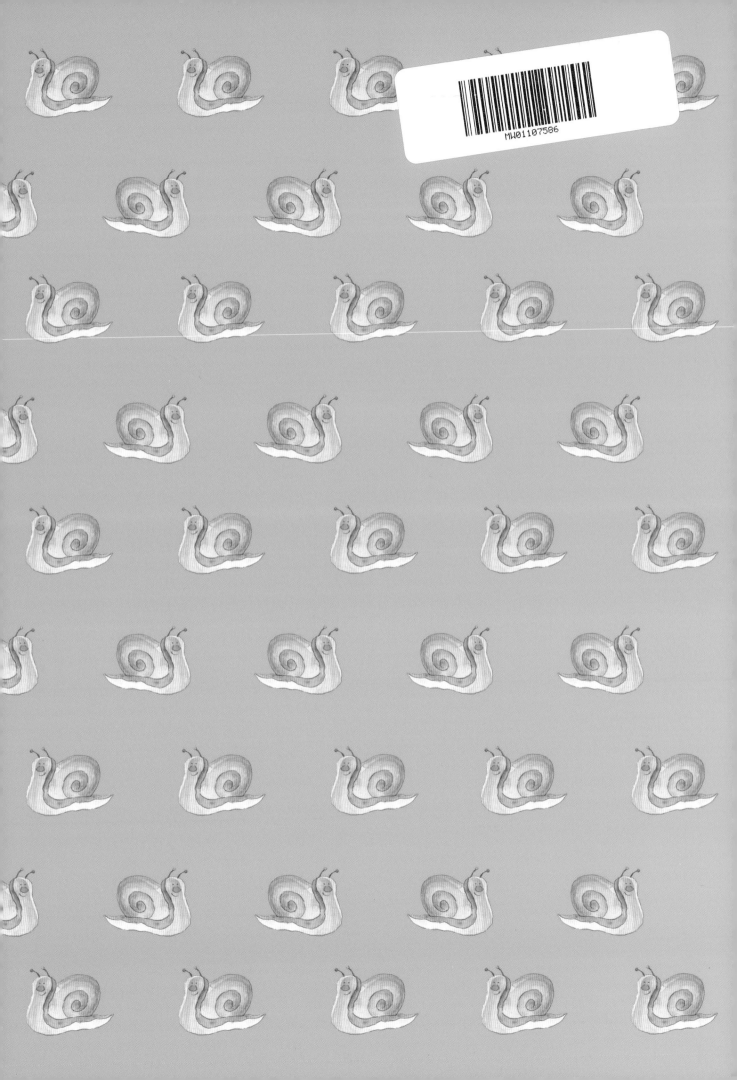

The Book Snail

Written by
Jin Bo

Illustrated by
Wang Zuming

CARDINAL
MEDIA

Text Copyright © Jin Bo
Illustration Copyright © Wang Zuming
Edited by Ellen Hunter Gans
English Copyright © 2018 by Cardinal Media, LLC.

978-1-64074-024-2

Printed in China

2 4 6 8 10 9 7 5 3 1

I am busy. Way too busy.

My parents sign me up for lots of different lessons.

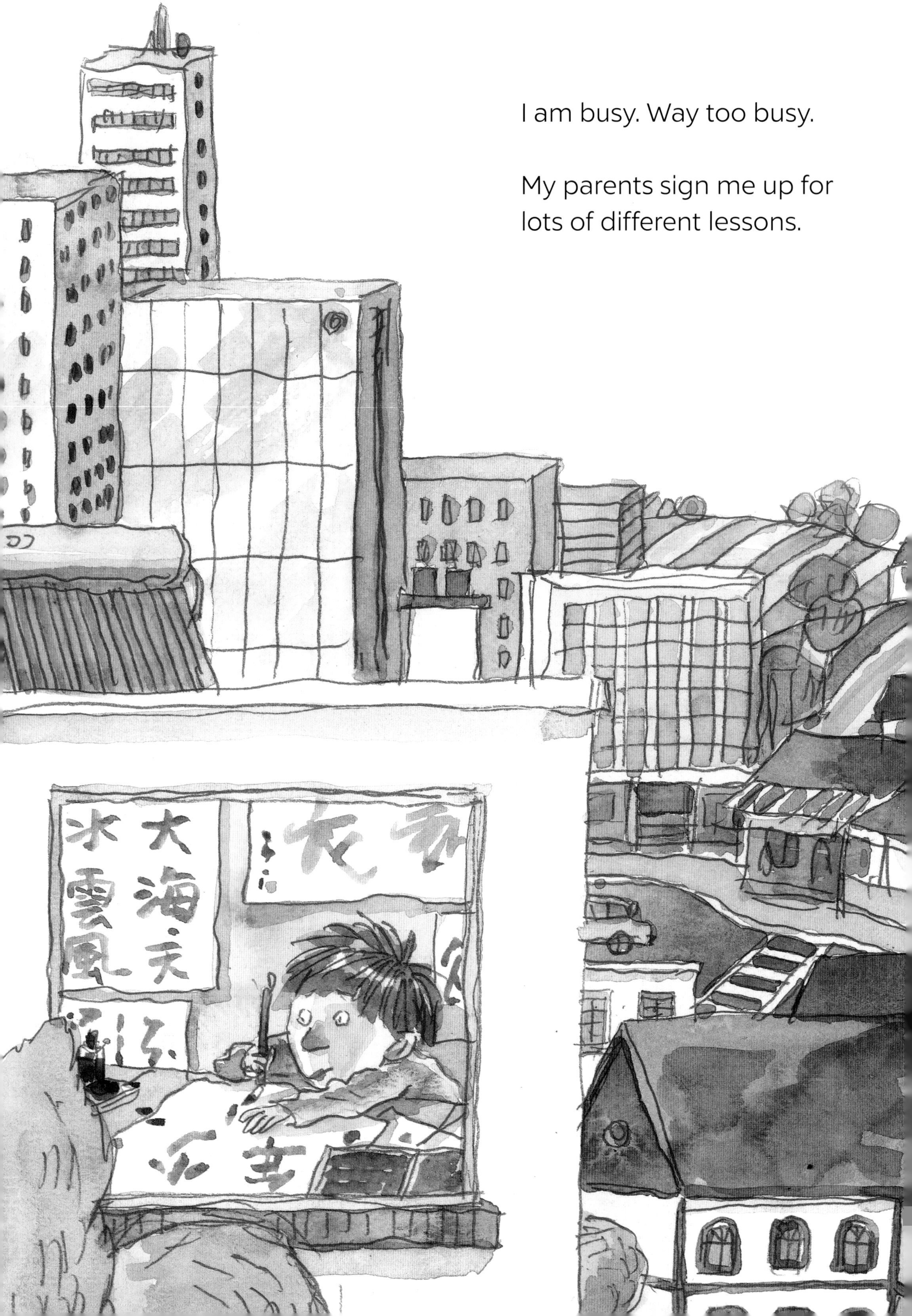
大海天
水雲風

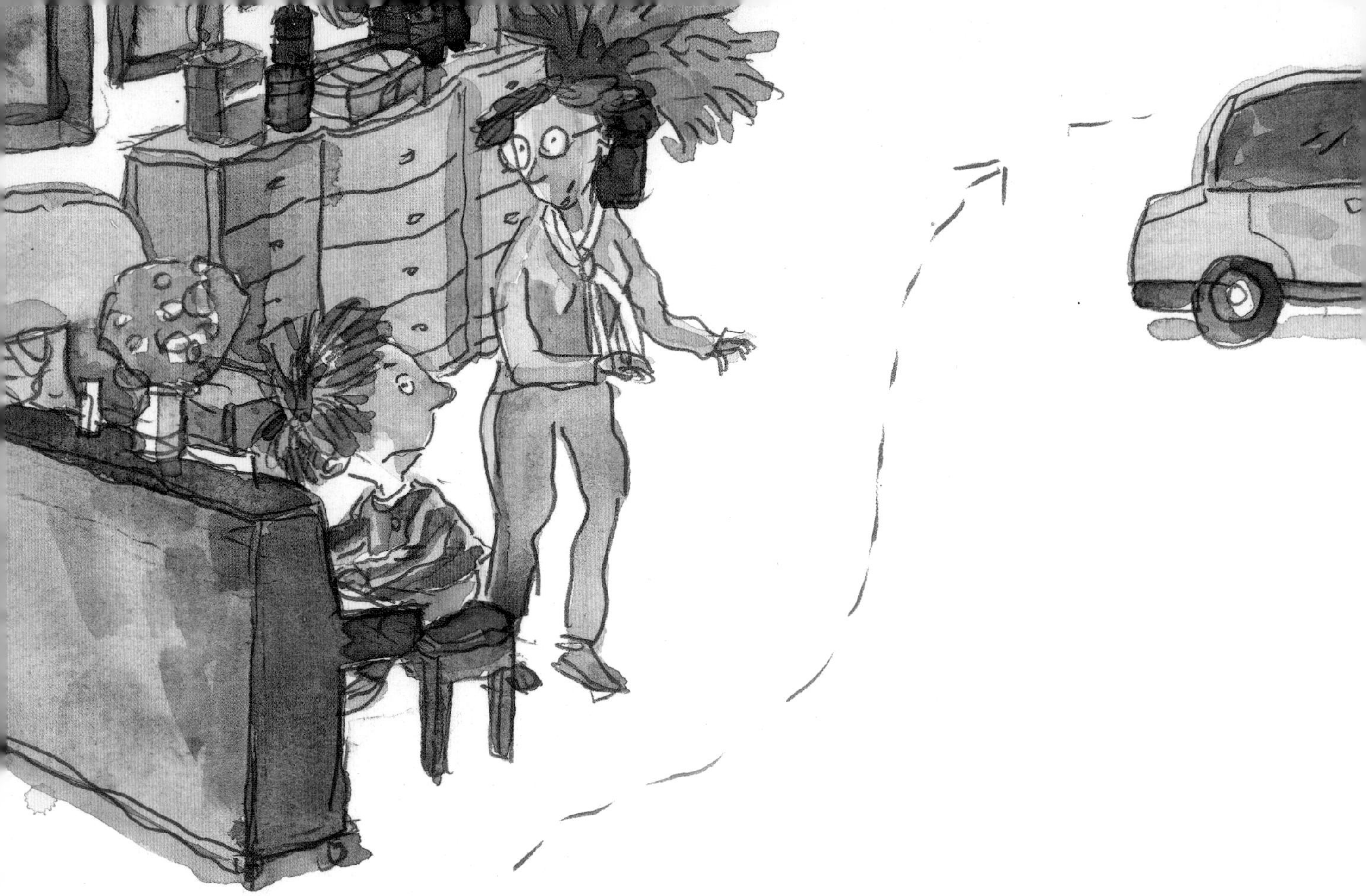

Piano lessons with Mrs. Li.

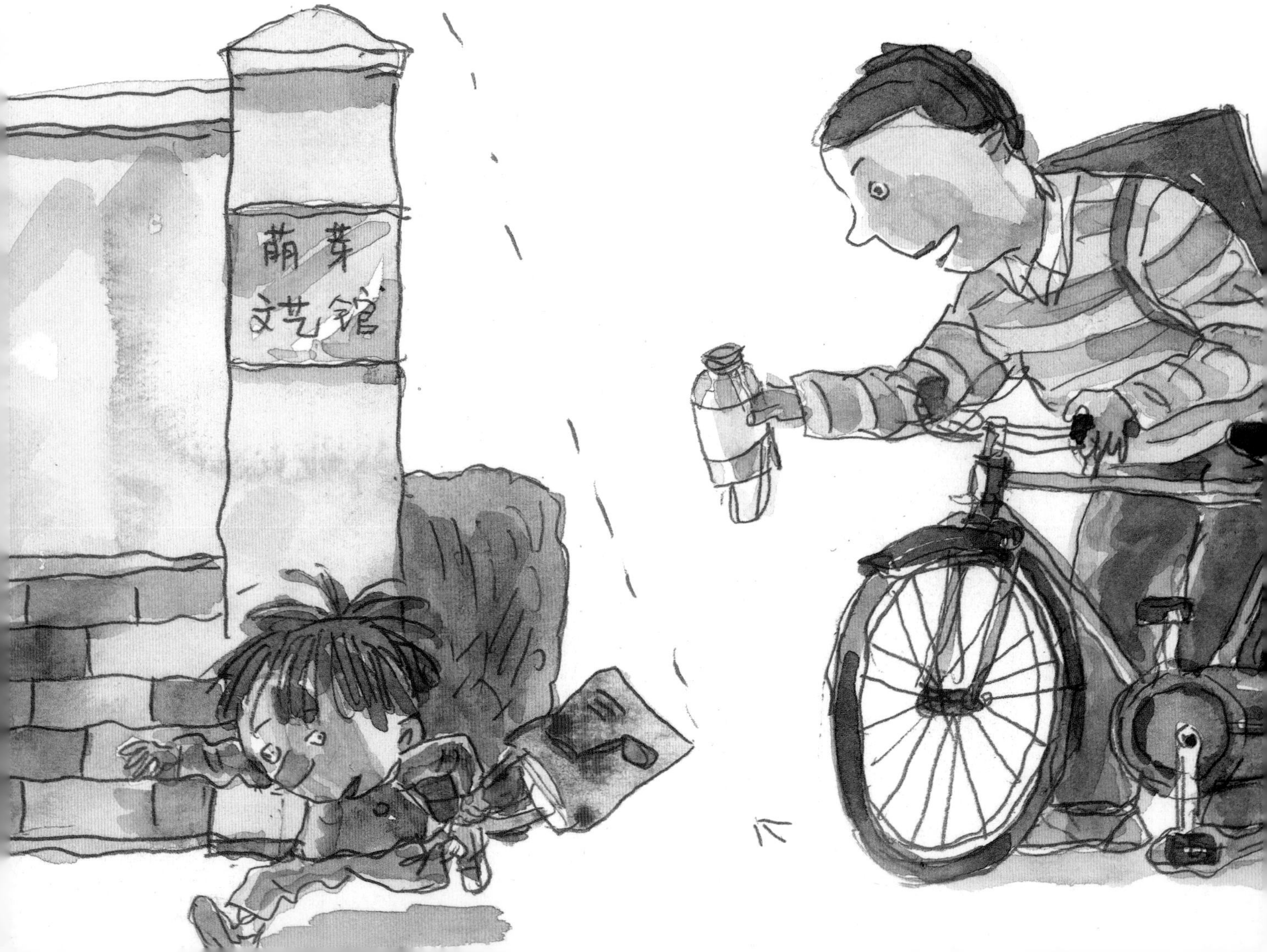
萌芽
文艺馆

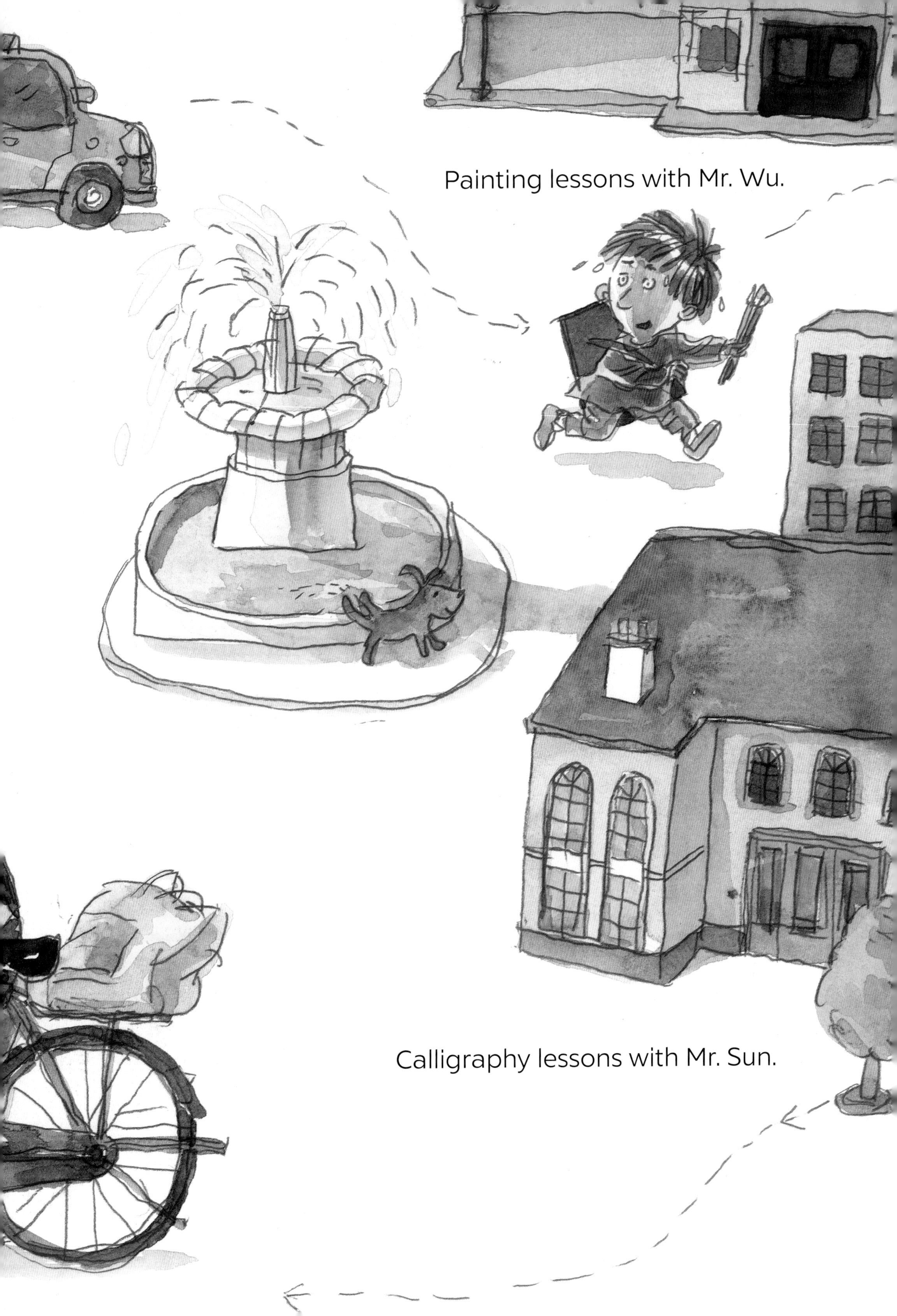

Painting lessons with Mr. Wu.

Calligraphy lessons with Mr. Sun.

I love learning, but I want to travel and go on big adventures!

Every time I ask Dad about taking a trip, he tells me to prepare for my lessons instead.

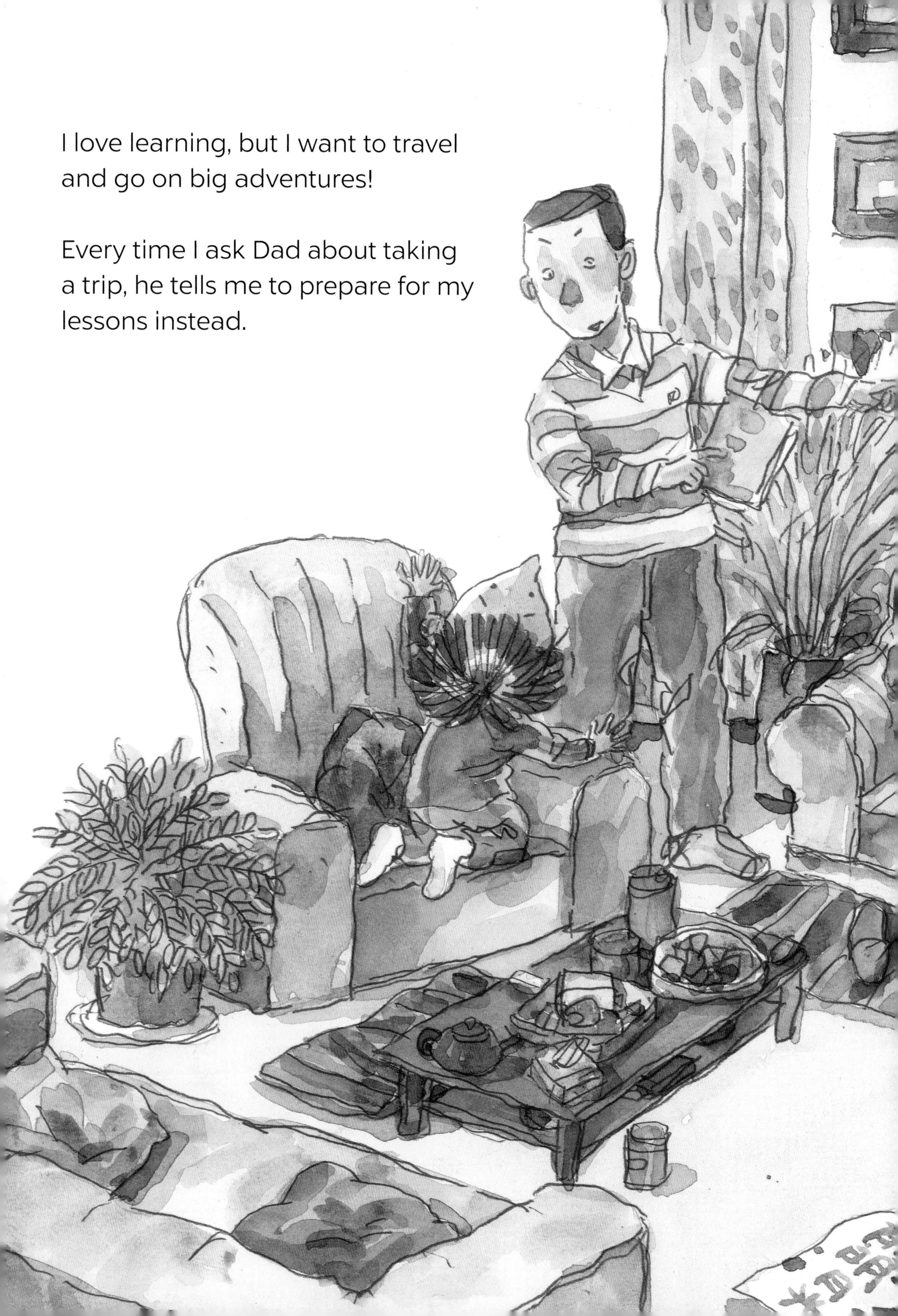

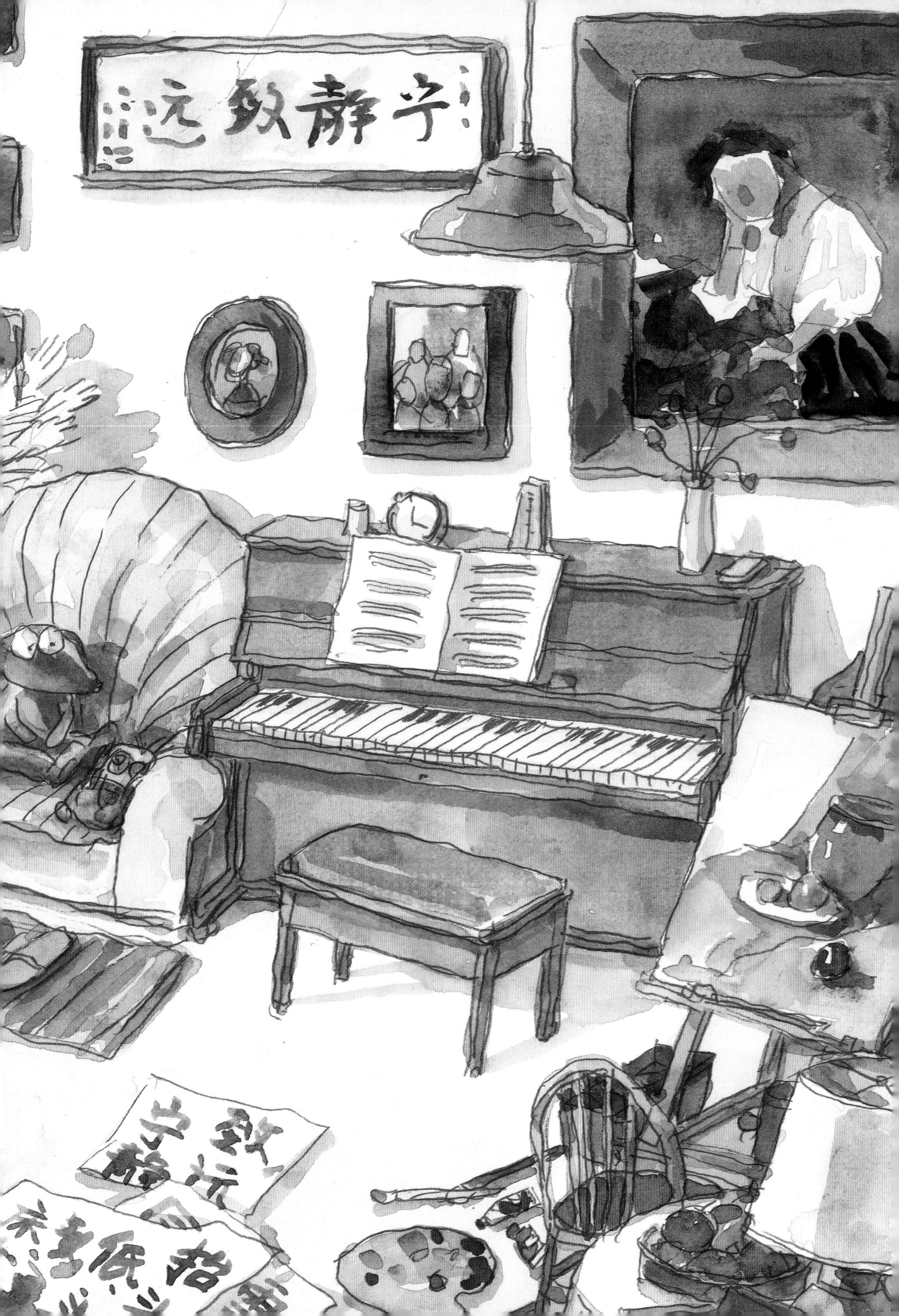
宁静致远

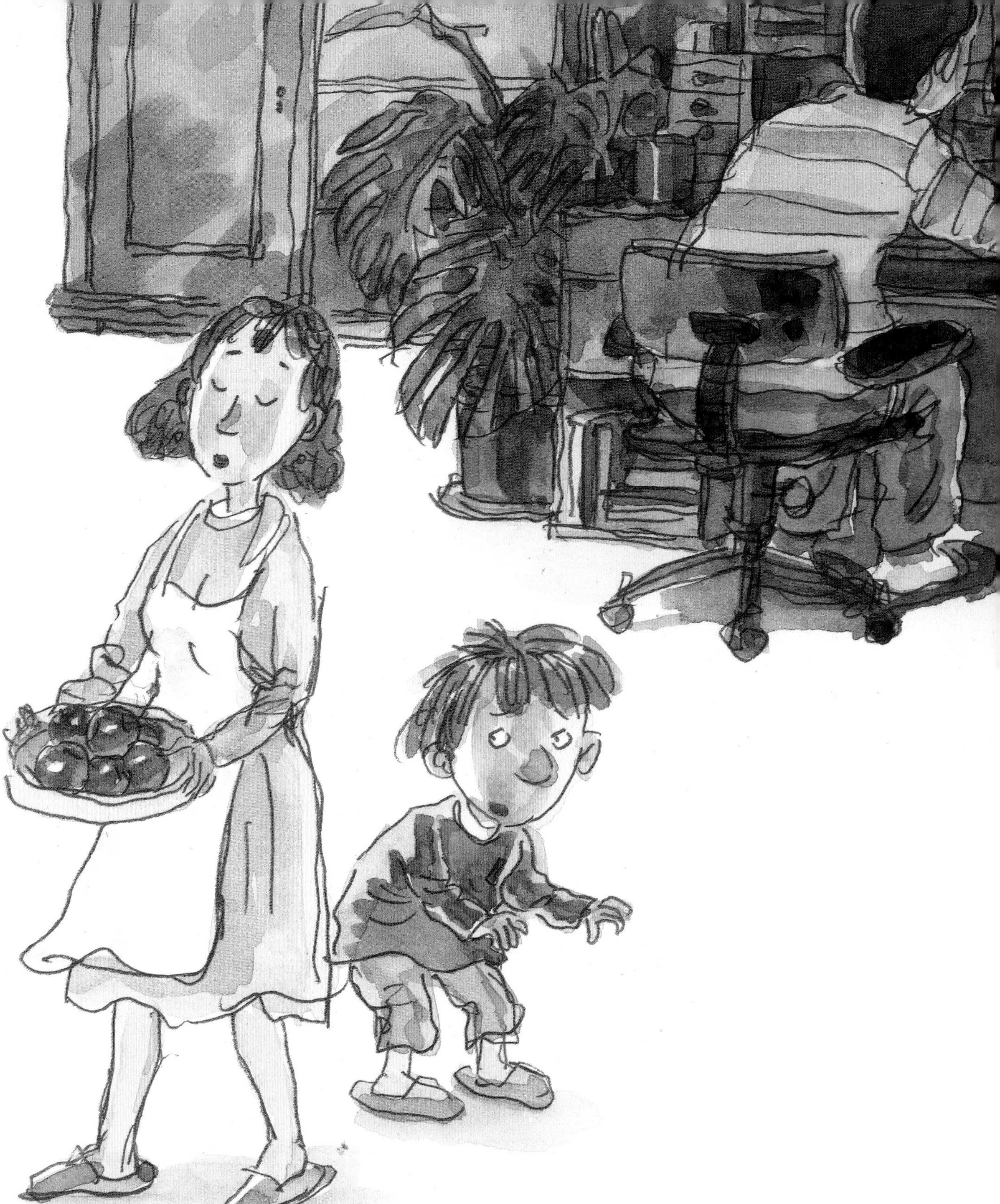

I asked Mom if I could go on an adventure.

And what did she say?

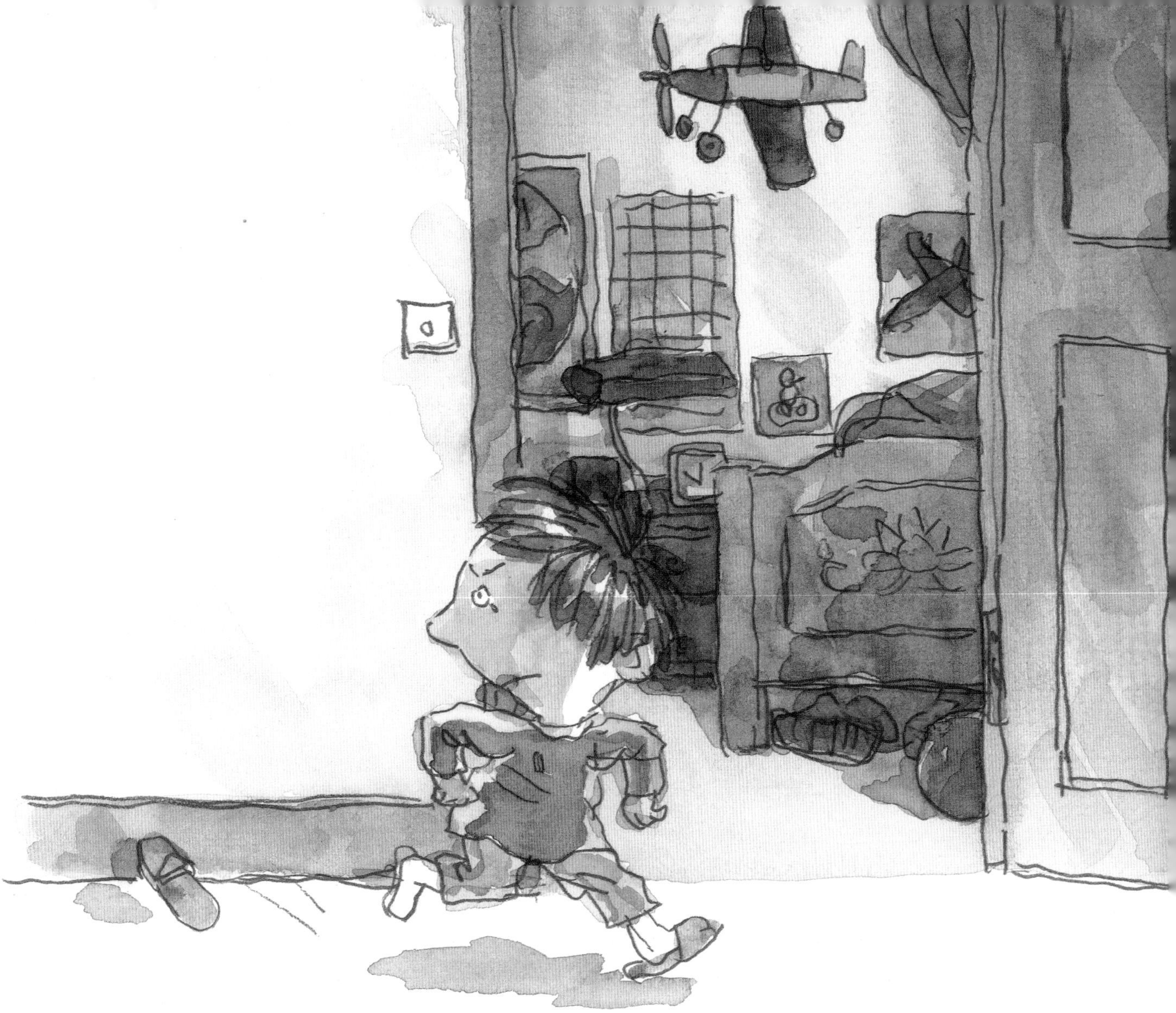

"It's time for bed."

I was so mad! No one listens to me around here!

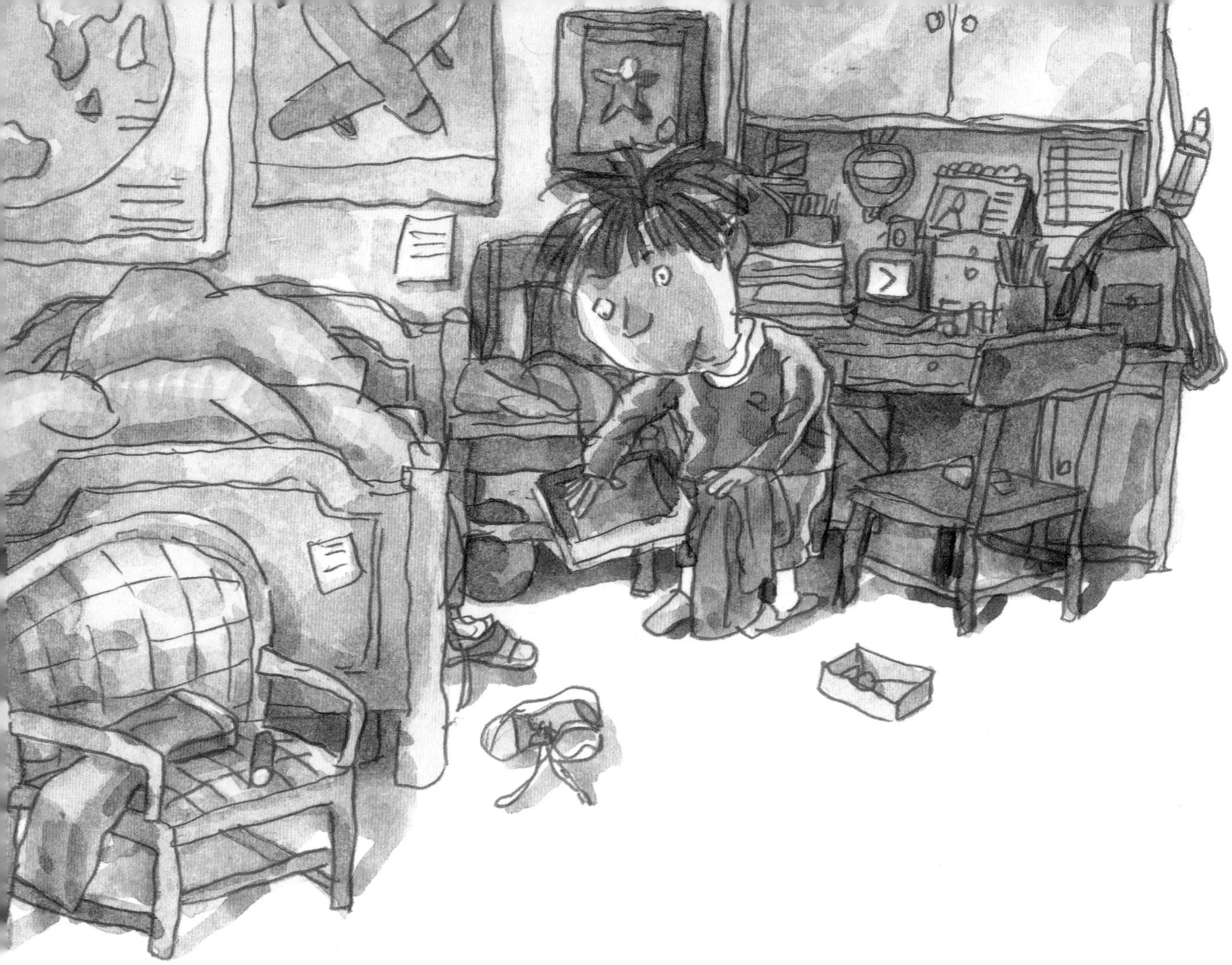

That night I noticed a book I'd never seen before.

It wasn't a schoolbook or a book for piano or painting or calligraphy.

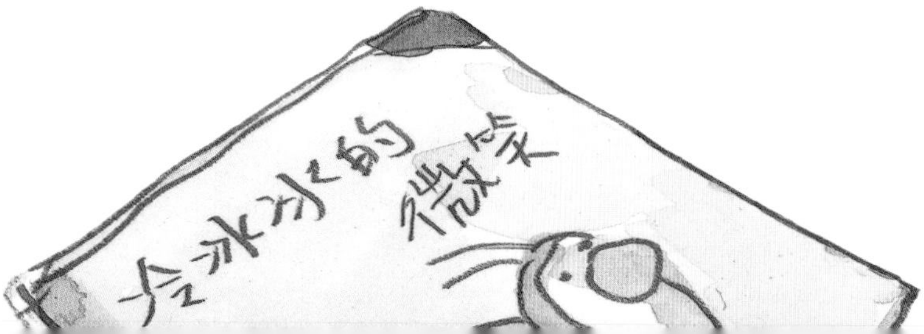

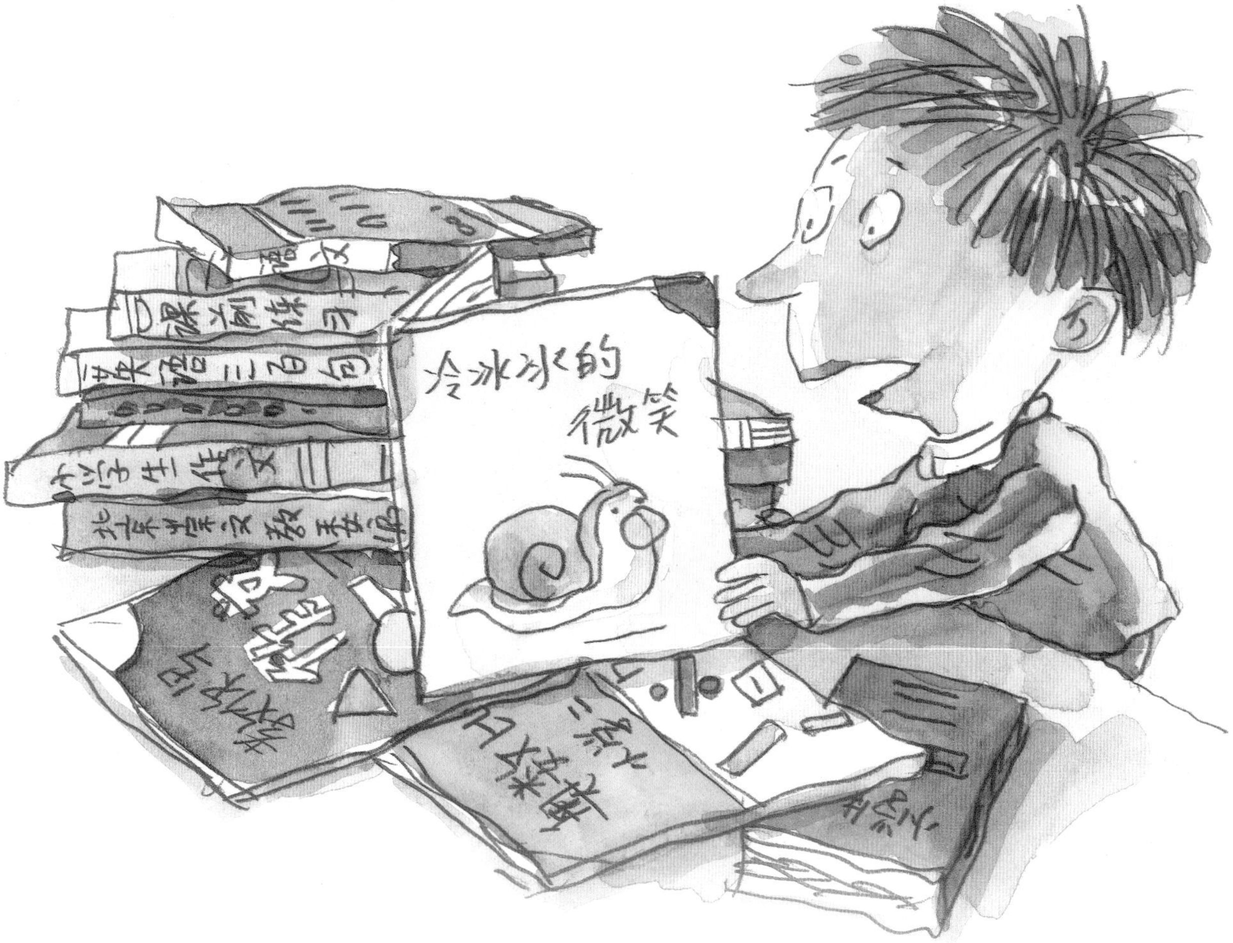
冷冰冰的
微笑

A snail was on the cover. I opened the book and read from one of its pages.

Snails have more than 14,000 teeth on their tongues.

"Teeth on the tongue?" I wondered out loud. Just then I heard a voice outside my window.

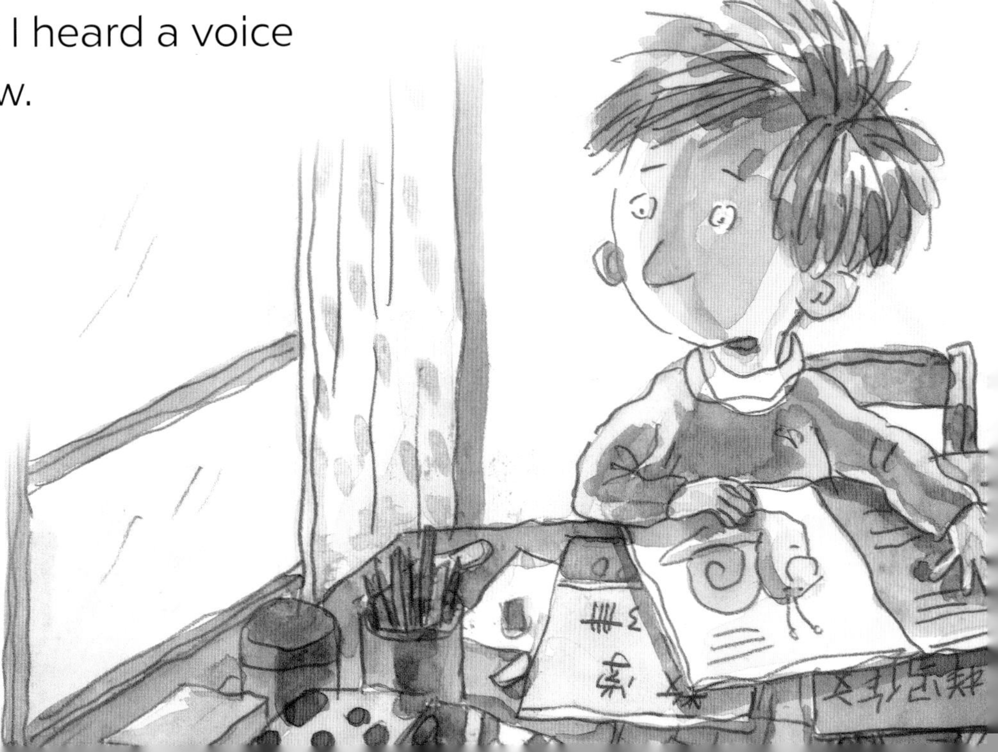

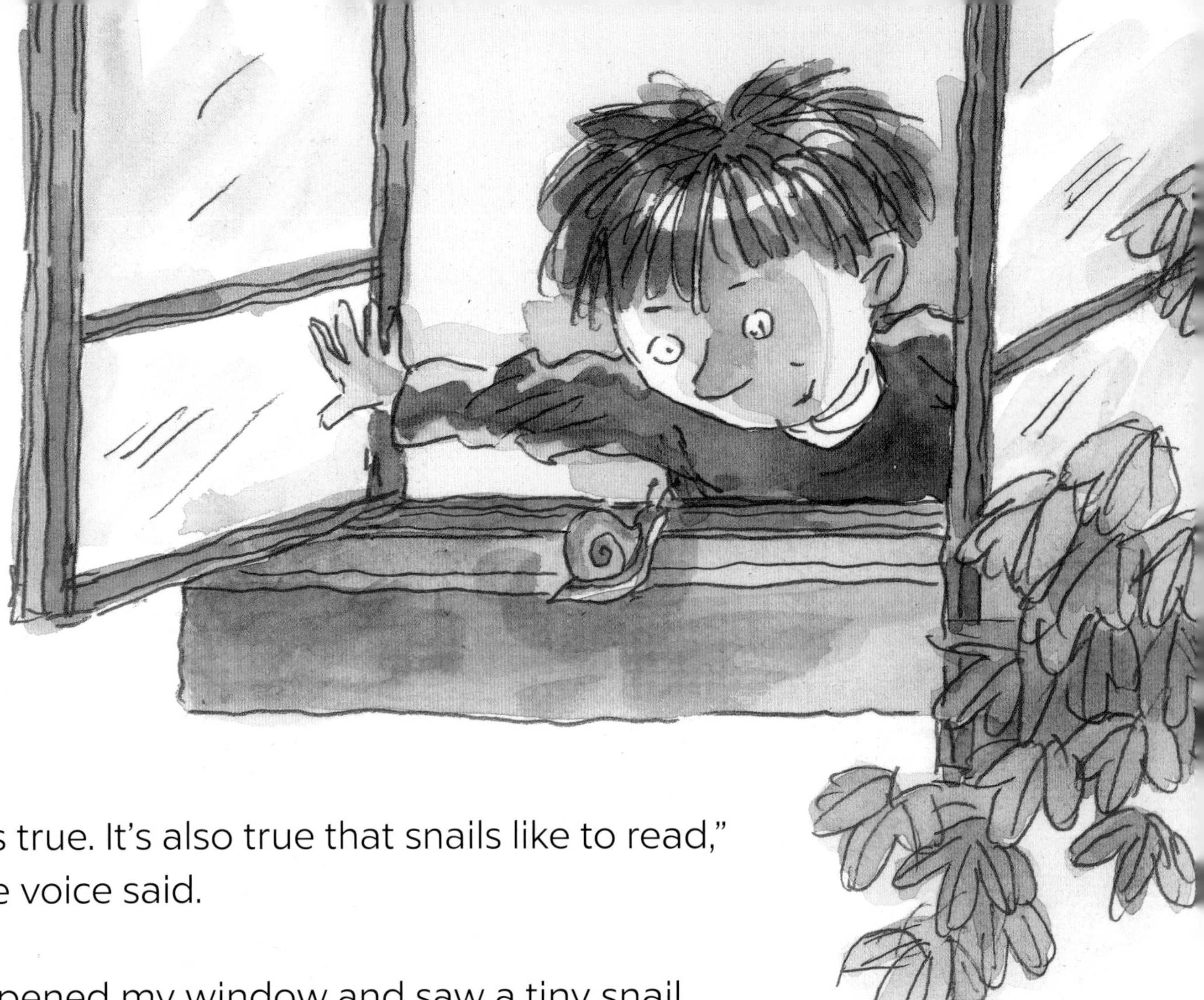

“It’s true. It’s also true that snails like to read,” the voice said.

I opened my window and saw a tiny snail crawling along my windowsill. A snail that had just talked to me!

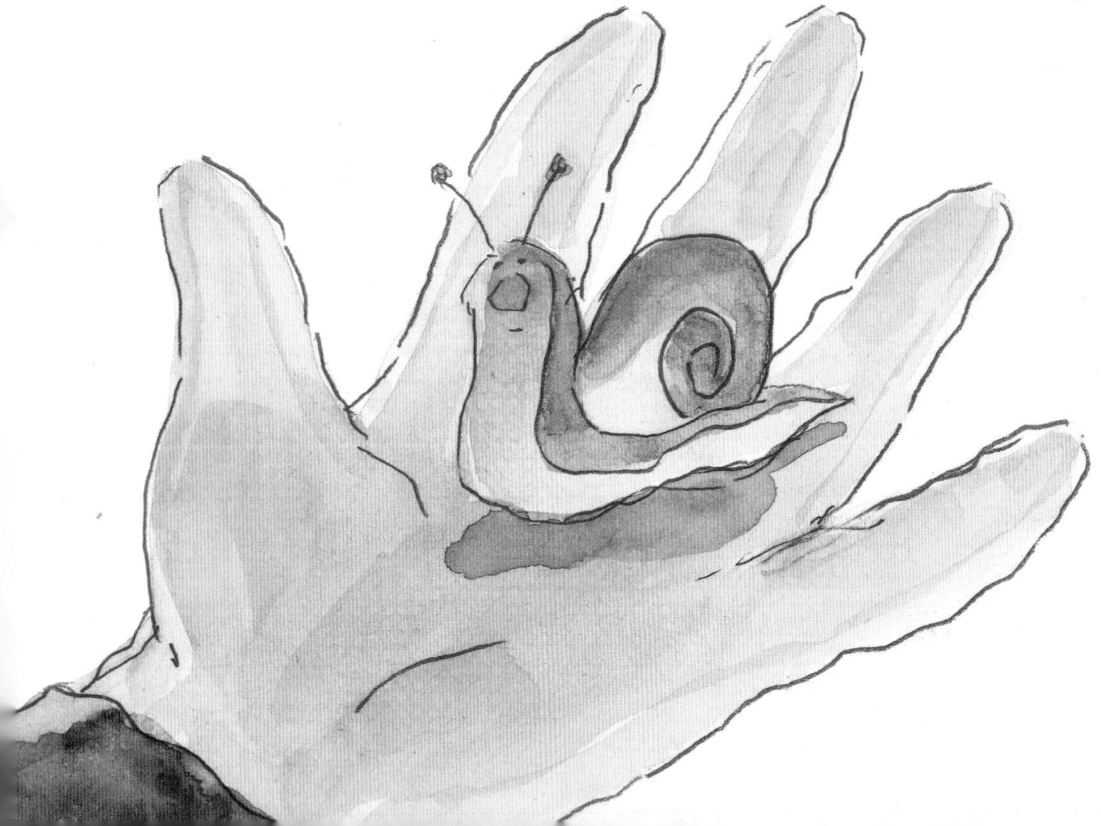

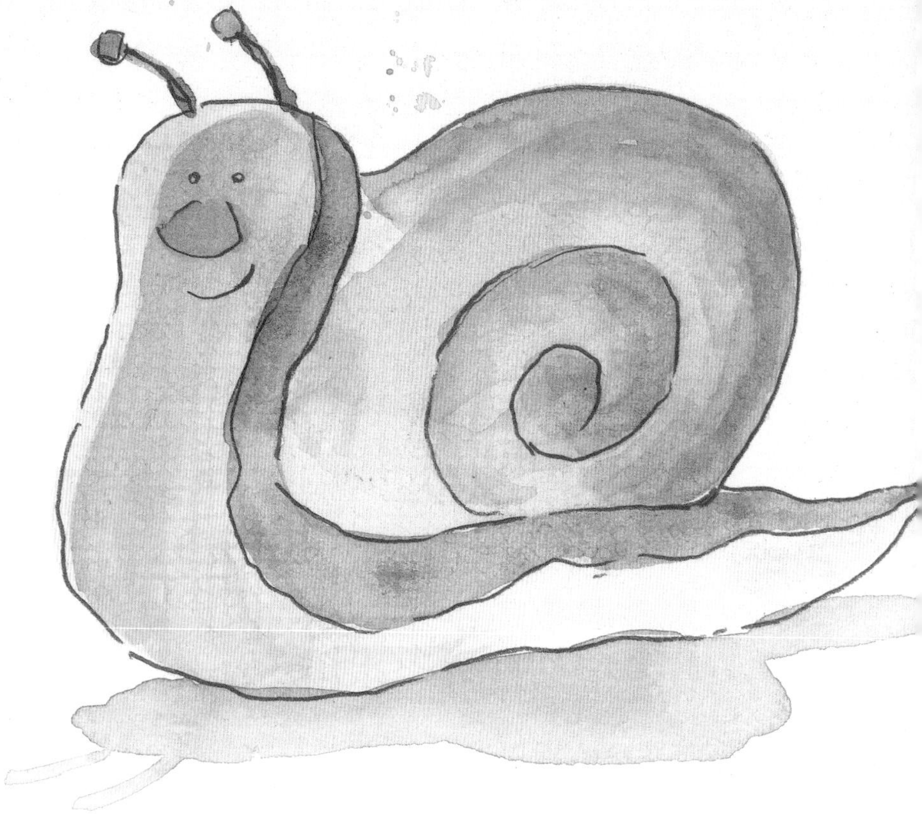

“I heard you talking about big adventures,” said the snail.
“I go on big adventures every time I read a book.”

This snail could talk *and* read? “I’ve heard of a book*worm* before, but never a book *snail*!” I told her.

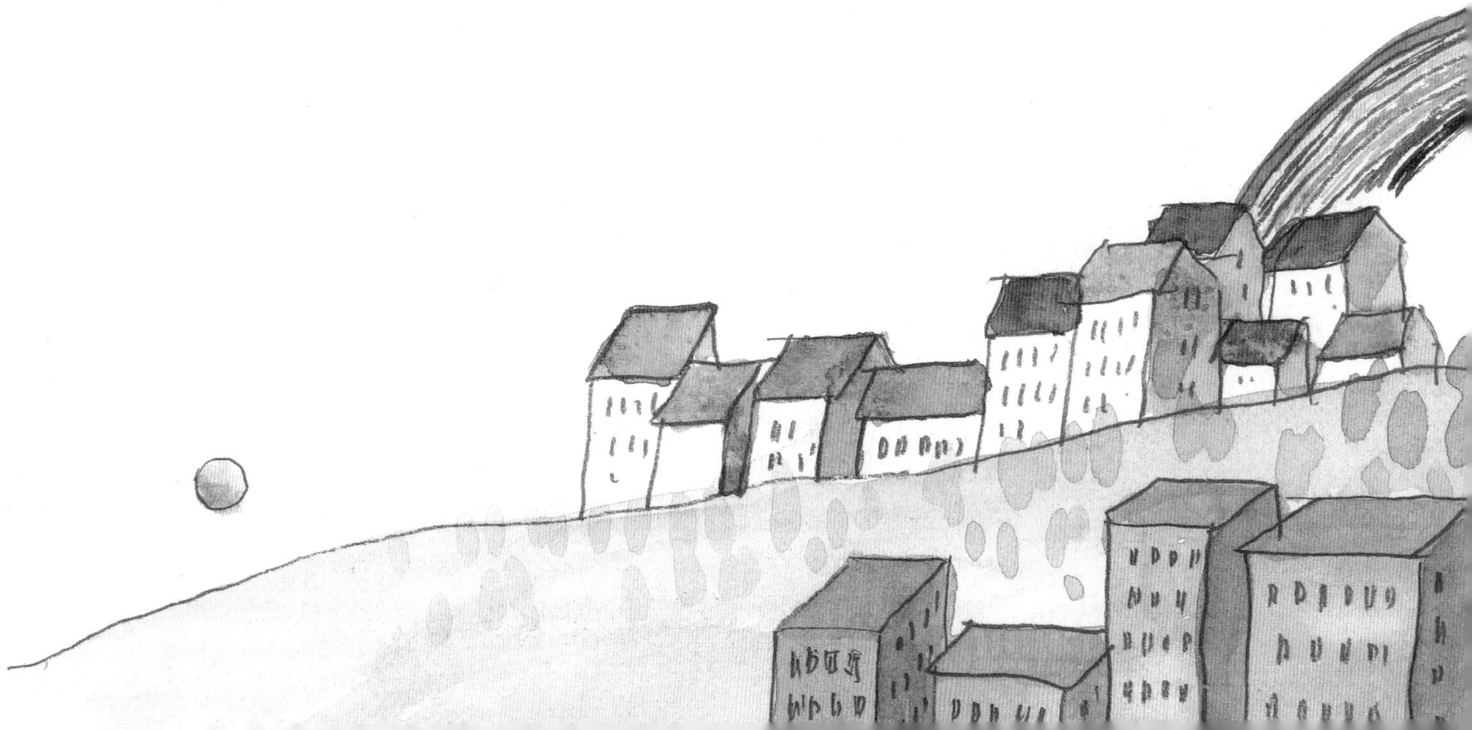

"I even have my very own library right here in my shell. Would you like to see it?" she asked.

Now *this* was the kind of big adventure I'd been waiting for. "Of course! But I can't fit in your shell," I told her.

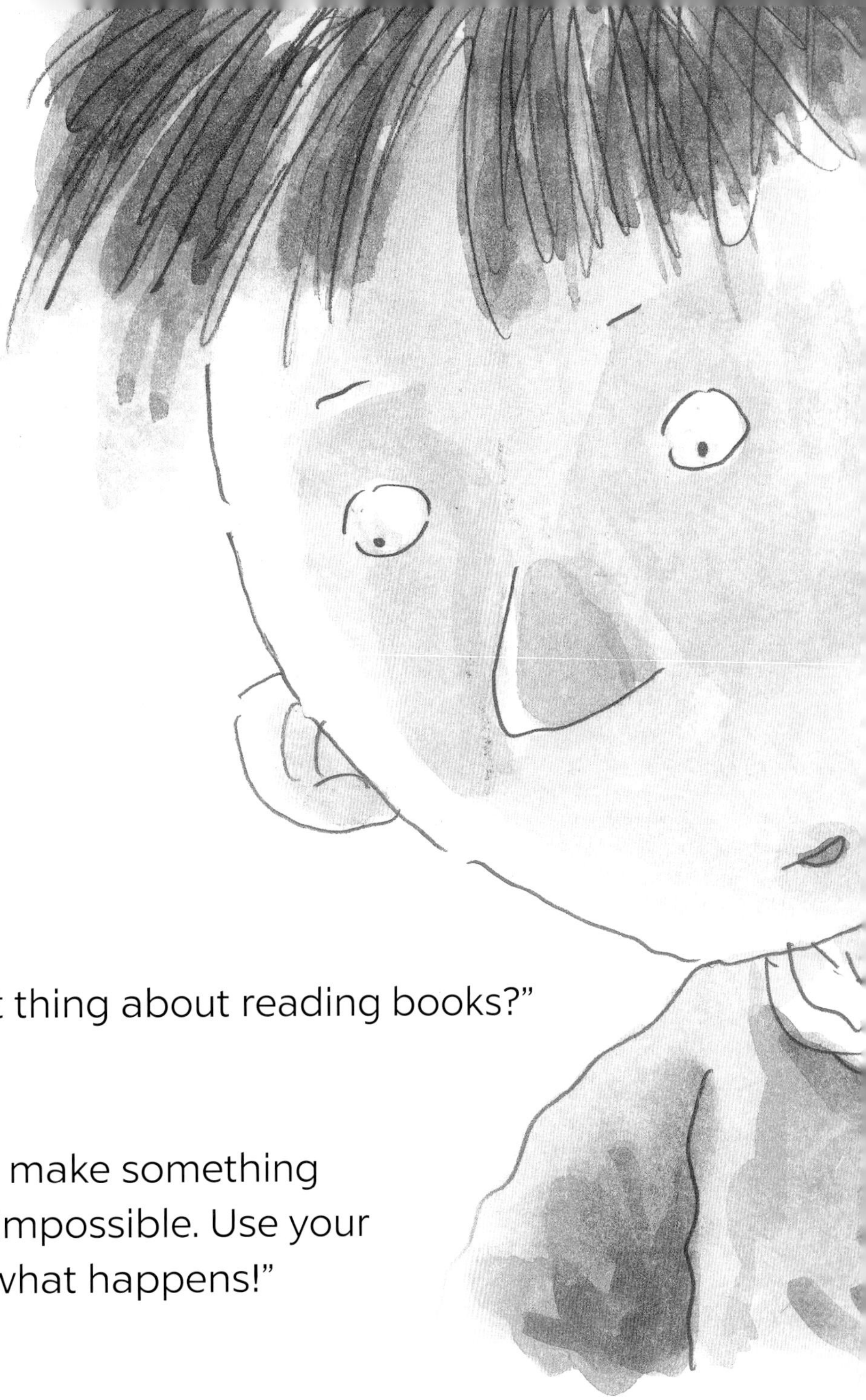

"Do you know the best thing about reading books?" the book snail asked.

"Your imagination can make something happen that seemed impossible. Use your imagination and see what happens!"

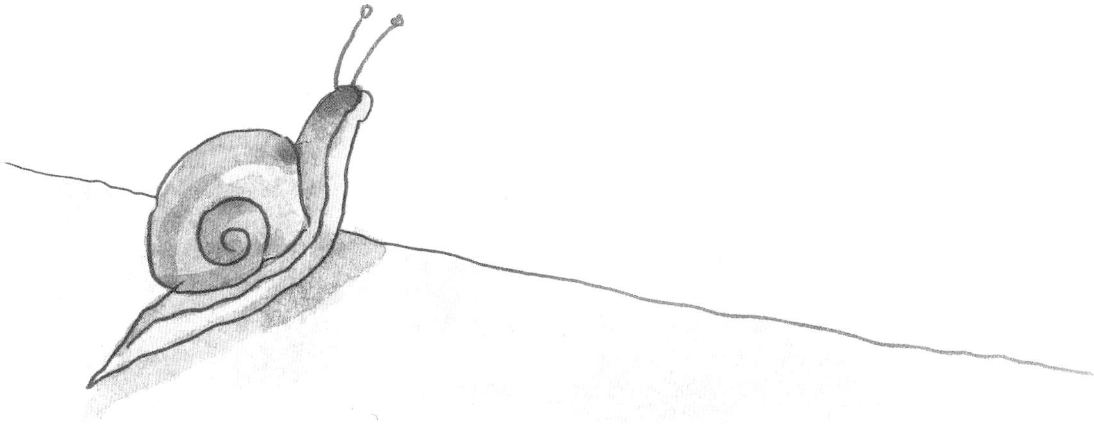

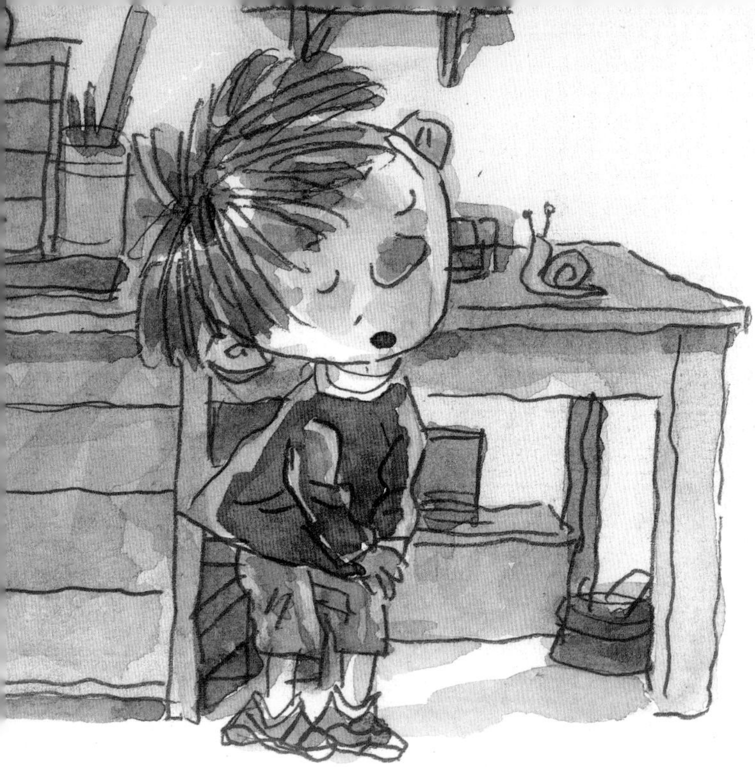

So I closed my eyes and whispered to myself, “Shrink, shrink, shrink…”

When I opened my eyes again—I was tiny! The book snail stood in front of me with a smile on her face.

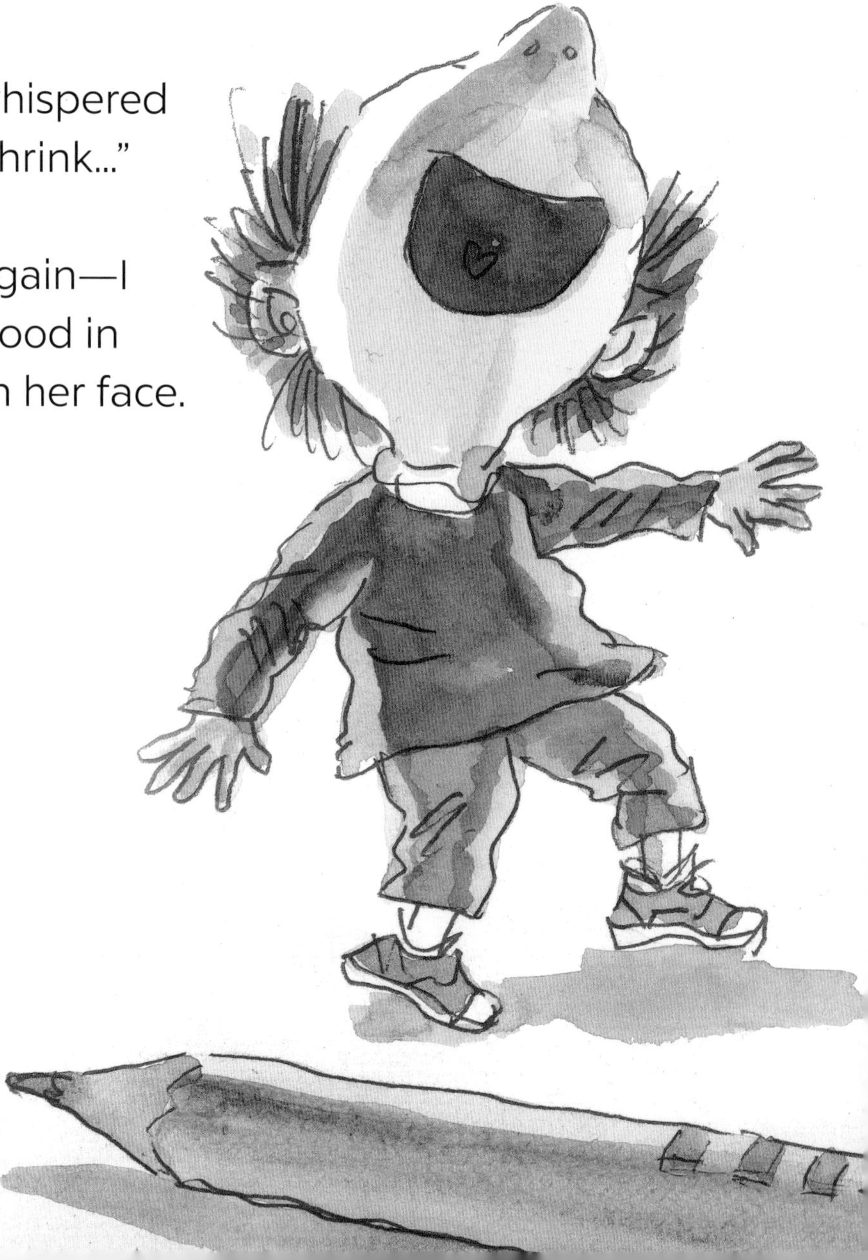

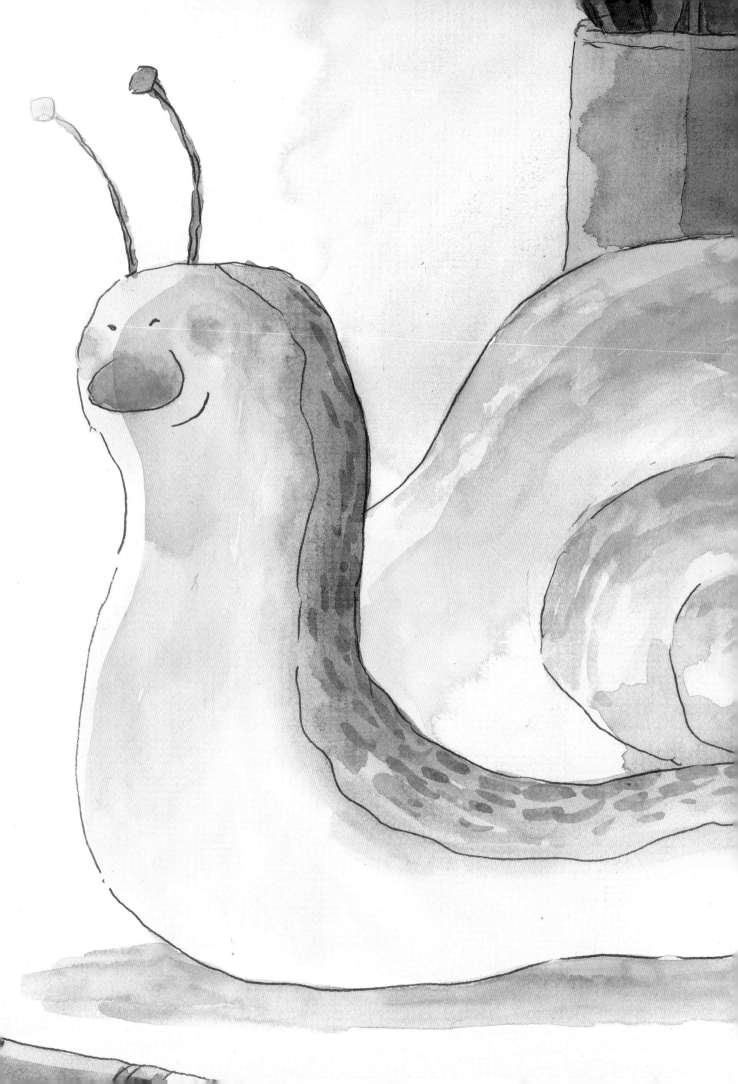

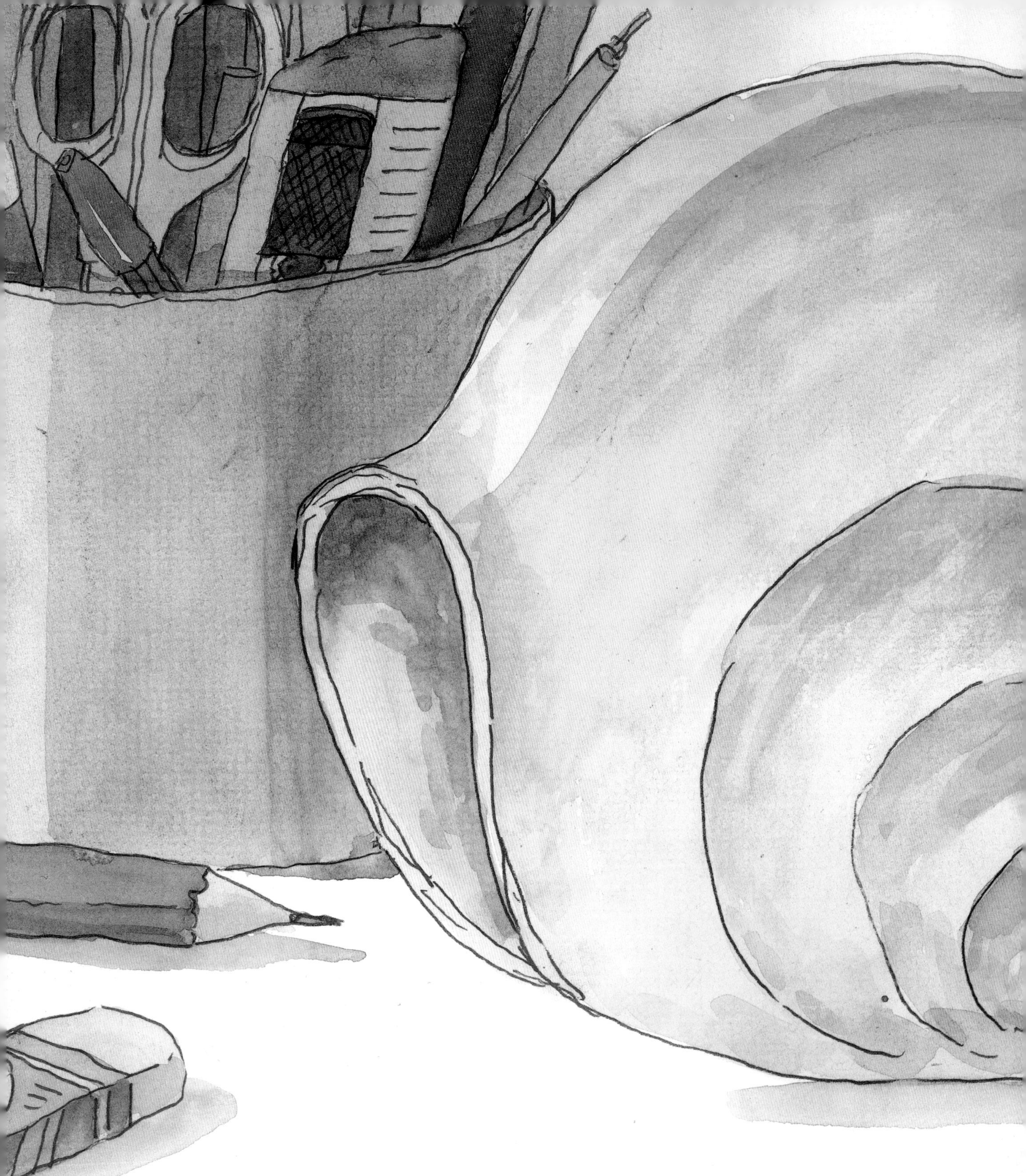

Then the book snail slid out of her shell.

“Welcome to my home,” she said.
“Please go right in.”

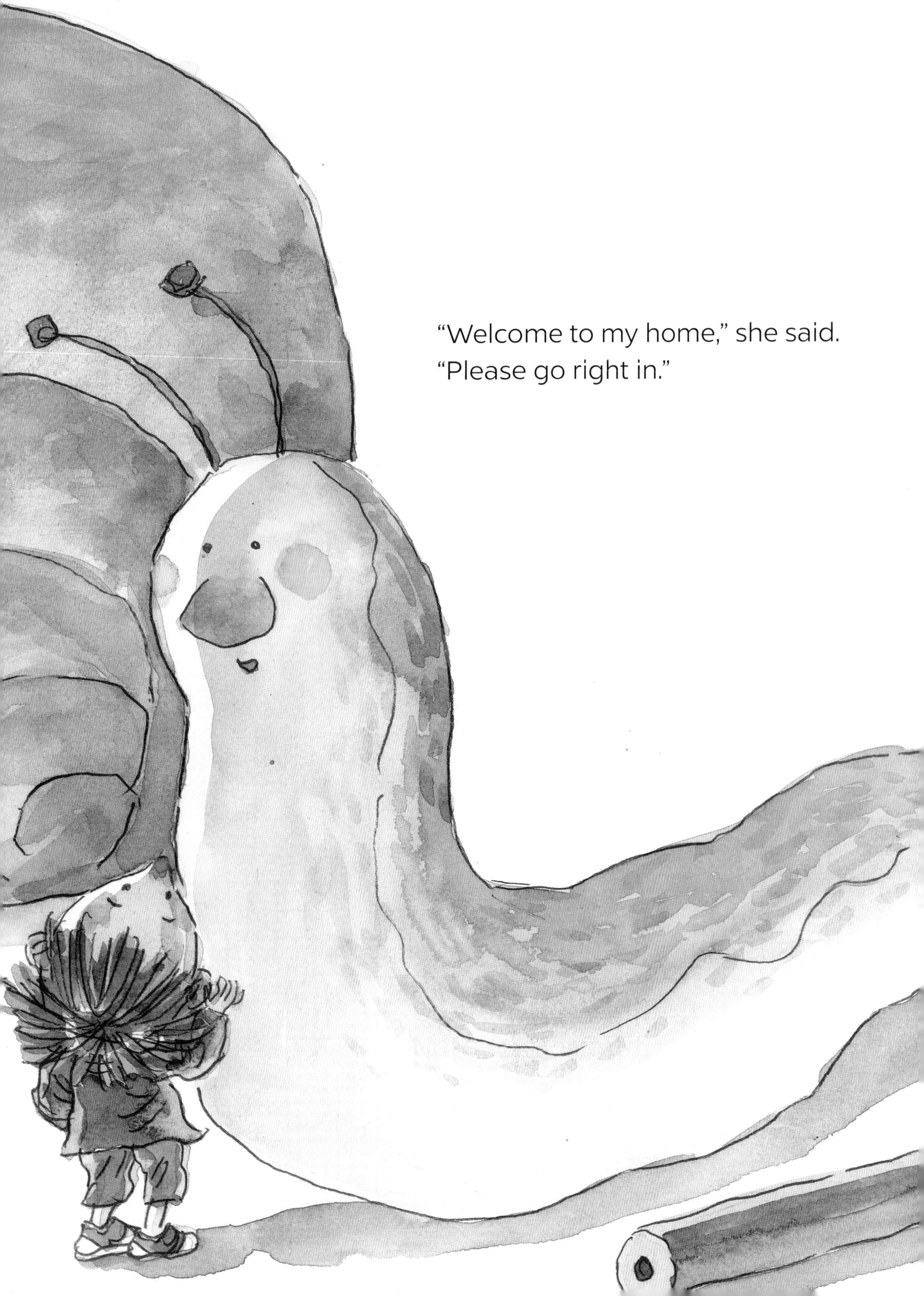

I walked inside and could hardly believe my eyes. Colorful artwork covered the walls. Rows of bookcases were full of books—all kinds of books.

This was the best big adventure *ever*.

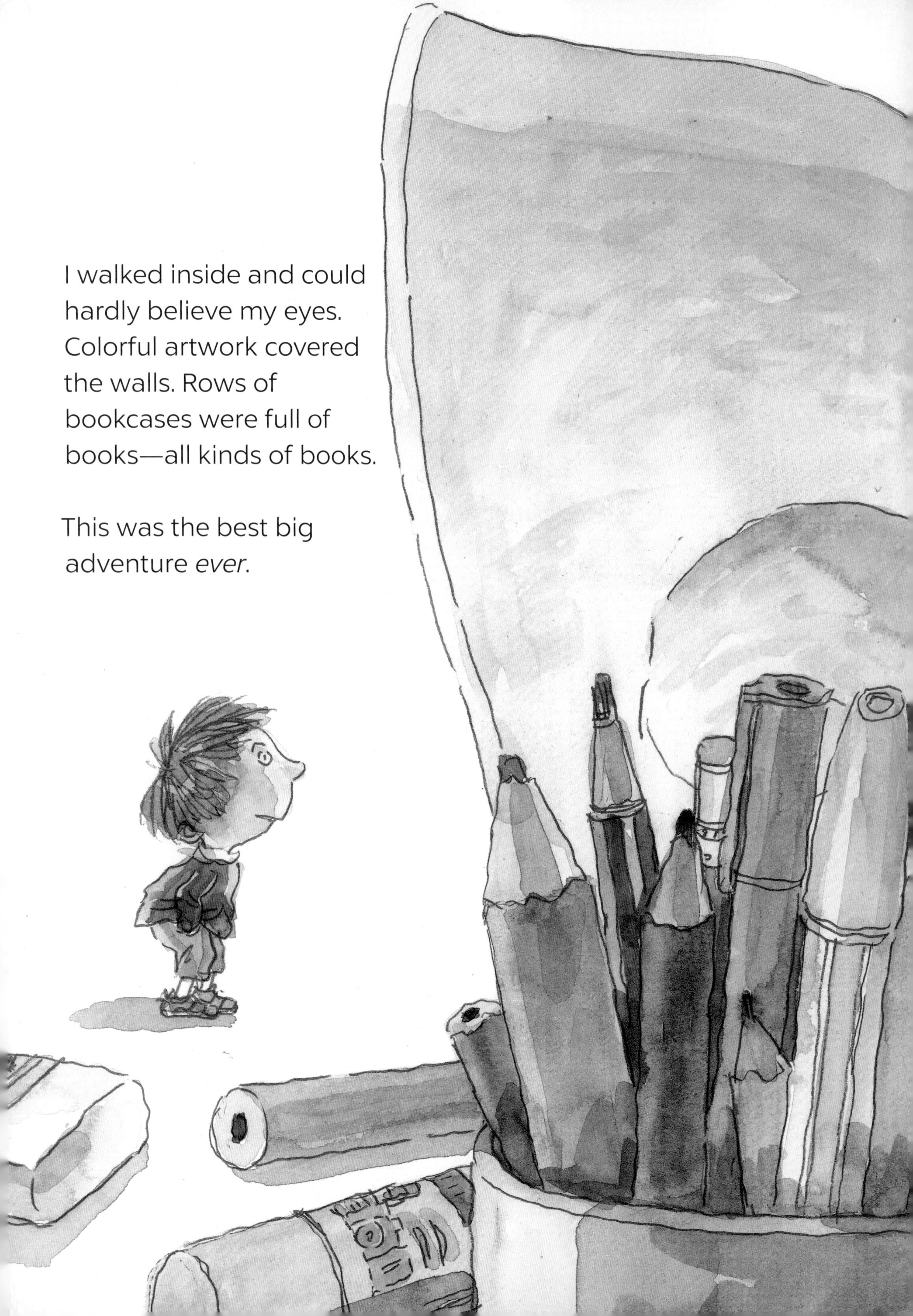

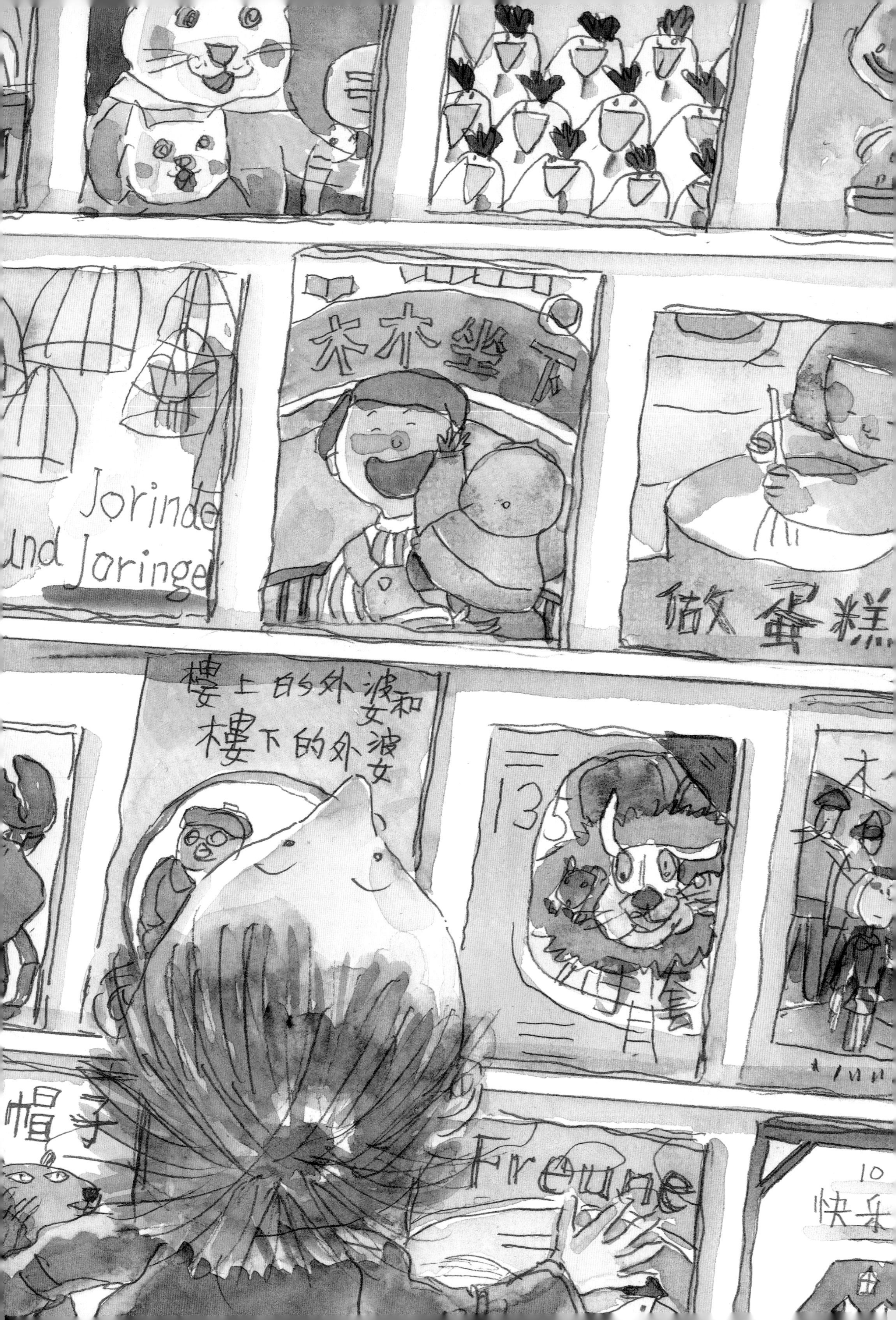

Jorinde und Joringel
做蛋糕
樓上的外婆和
樓下的外婆
135
帽子
Freune
10
快乐

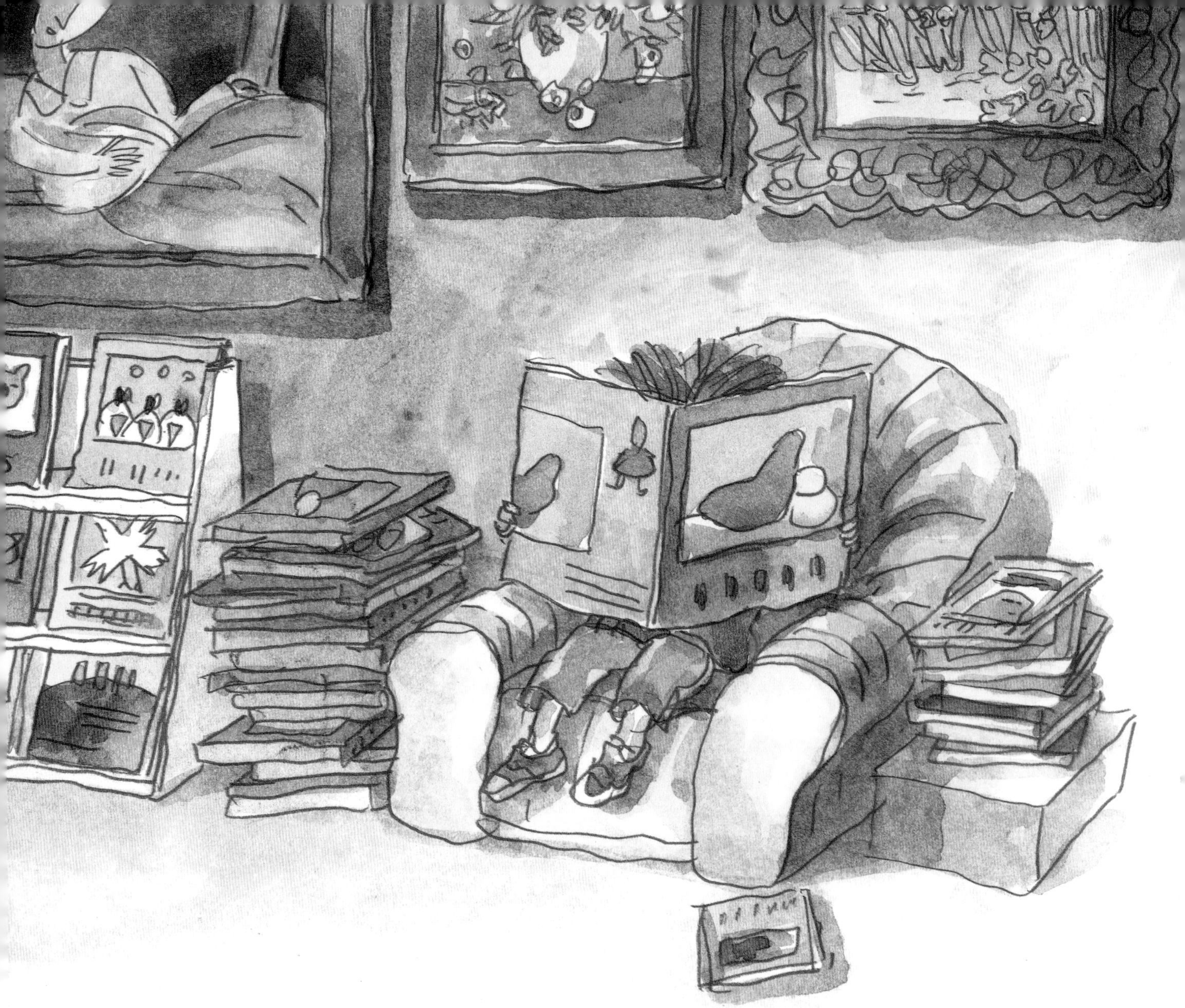

I pulled a book off the shelf and sat down to read. I finished it and read another and then another. I knew I should get home but I was afraid I'd never have another adventure like this.

Then I heard the book snail's voice again: "When you read books, you can have a big adventure anytime you want."

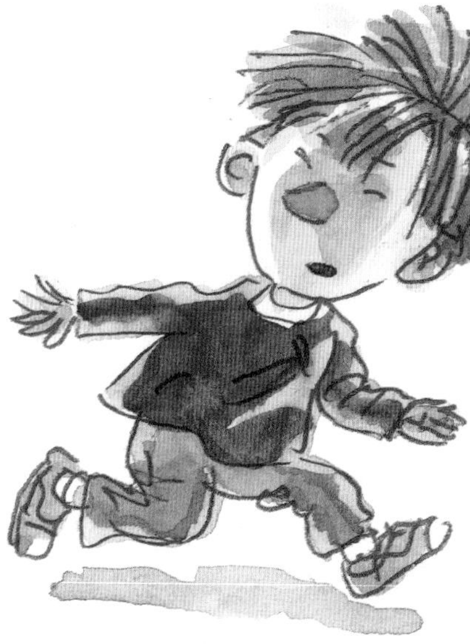

The book snail was right.

I imagined myself big and grew back to my normal size.

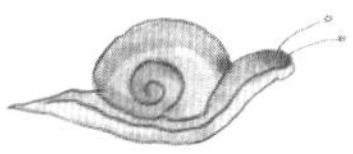

Then I started reading books all the time. And not just the books for my lessons. I read books about all kinds of big adventures.

And in my imagination, a tiny snail went with me on each one.

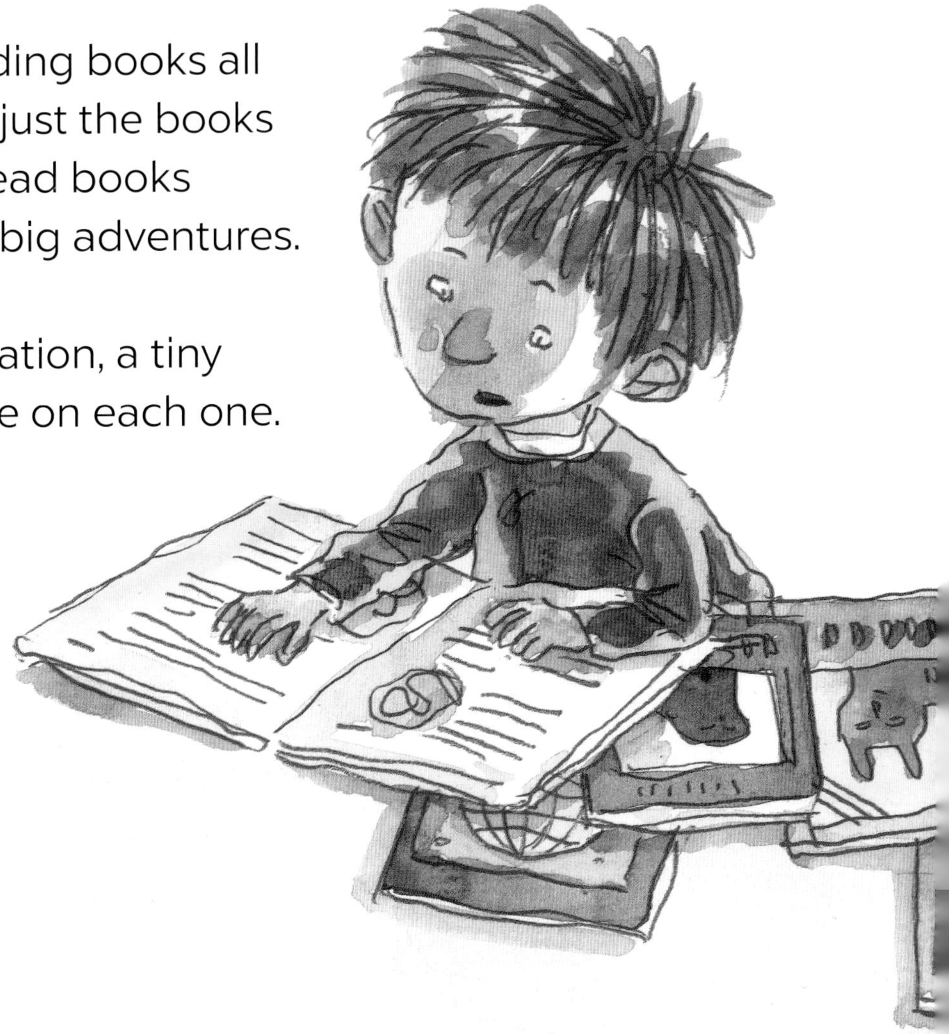

I don't mind all of my lessons so much anymore.

I know that after piano and painting and calligraphy, I can go on any adventure I want. I've even thought about making up my own big adventures by writing my own books.

Maybe I'll start by telling a story about a book snail...

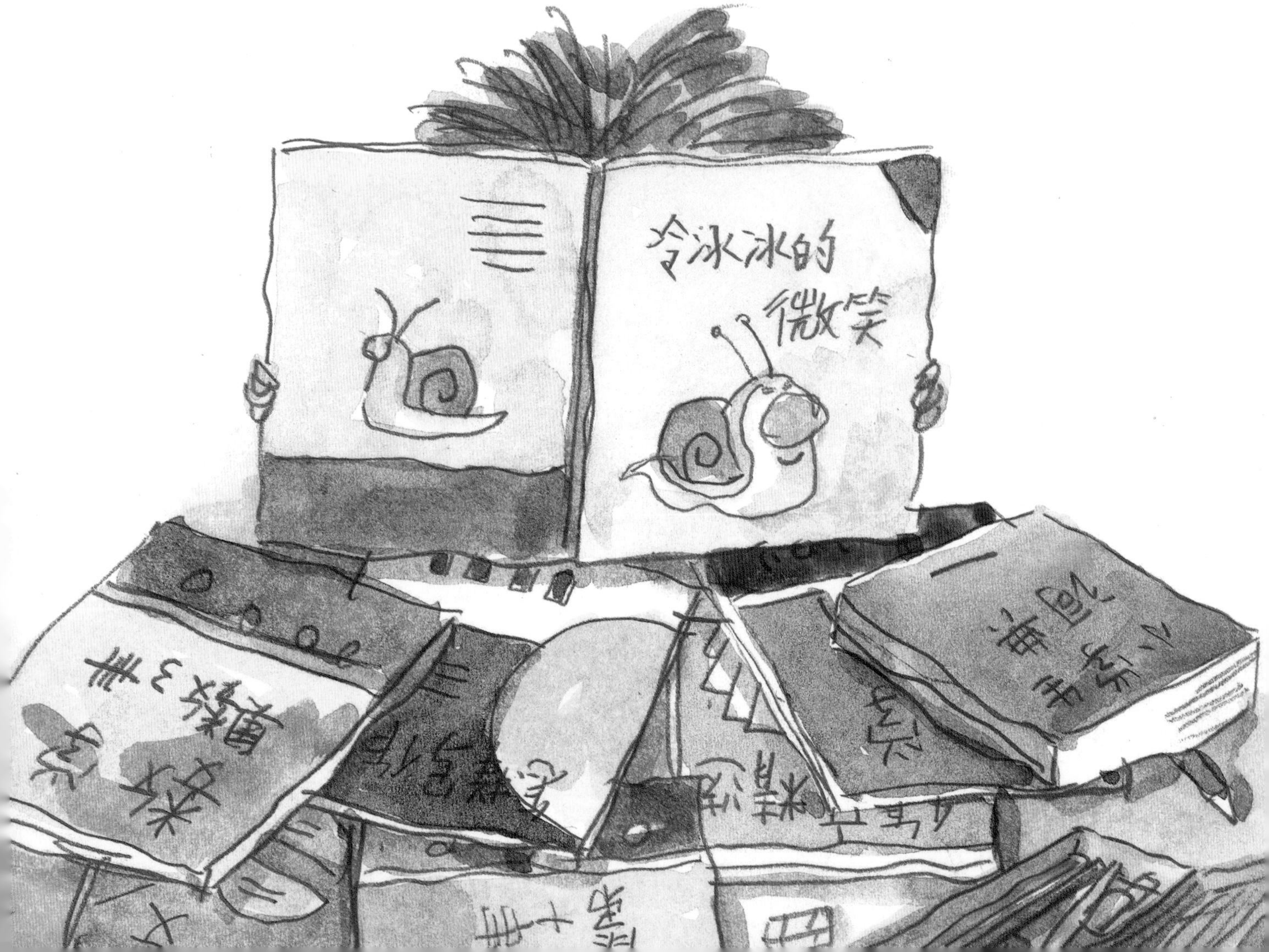
冷冰冰的
微笑

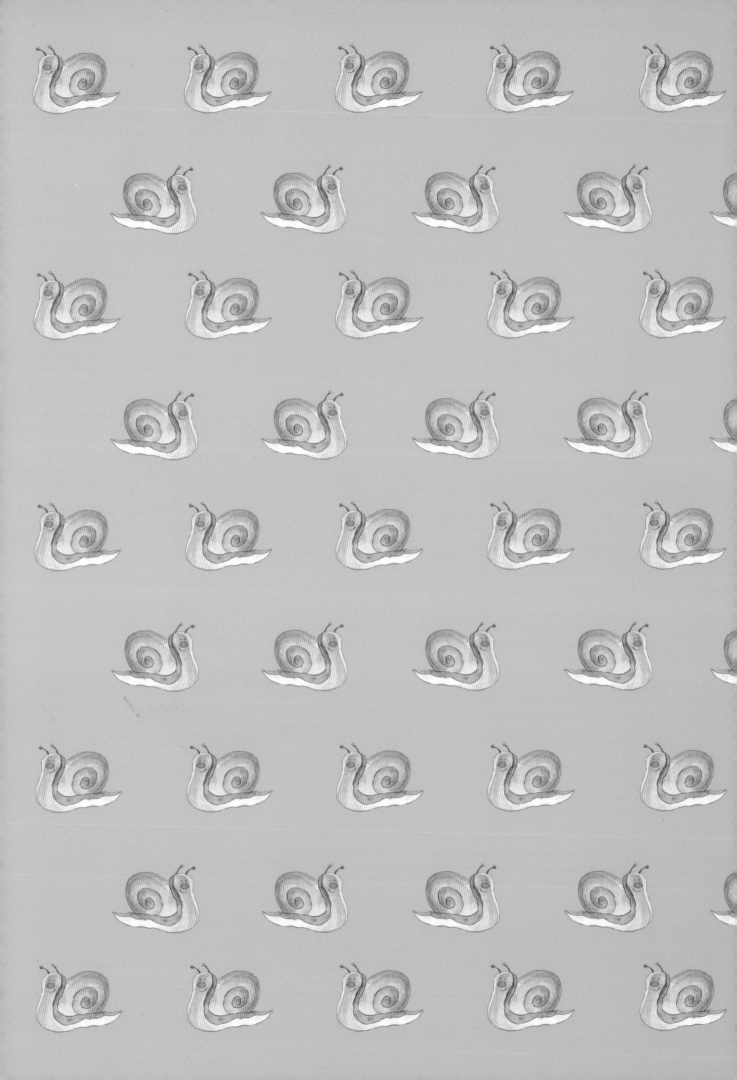